MONSTER
FARTS

WRITTEN AND ILLUSTRATED BY
JANE BEXLEY

ISBN 9798459027686

If you met a monster would you run or would you stay? Fangs and claws and furry paws would frighten most away.

But monsters aren't scary, at least not how you think.
It's their farts that should be feared, they are big and loud
and stink!

Vampires are quiet and sneaky and strong,
and so are the toots they squeak out all night long.

Their scariest parts aren't their
fangs, don't you see?
It's the gas flapping their capes
that should scare you and me.

Bigfoot roams through the forest with freedom to vent
all the gas that he wants with his big sasquatch scent.
He hides in the trees fumigating his foes,
so if you want to find him, just follow your nose!

The silent but deadlies surprise us the most
and they are the specialty of every ghost.
Those spooks can float by without being seen
and gas a whole room, then get away clean.

Witches are tricksters in black hats and boots.
Sometimes they cast silly spells on their toots.
They'll charm their fart clouds to smell flowery sweet
or curse a stink bomb as a trick, not a treat.

The kraken is known as the beast of the sea
and he cracks more than ships when he sets his gas free

That thunderous boom doesn't strike in the skies,
the gas blasts from below to the sailors' surprise.

Most spooky creatures can toot without care,
but Frankenstein's monster has to beware.
A big smelly fart just might lead to his doom
if the blow pops a seam when his bum needs to boom.

Eating nothing but brains isn't good for your guts and makes zombies produce stinky smells from their butts.

While they have lots of toots, they don't have lots of smarts.
So they wander around having bum and brain farts.

Nessie is shy and she stays down below
the waves of Loch Ness as they drift to and fro.

She toots booty bubbles that float to the top
and release cloudy gas as they surface and pop.
(If she needs to come up, she just hides in her mist
so that everyone thinks that she doesn't exist.)

How did the moon become covered in craters?
Just ask aliens who shoot stinky vapors.

They love to bounce on their bums and make clouds of moon dust. Extraterrestrial farts have some high-powered thrust!

Mummies are buried in tombs made of stone.
So how do they lift that huge lid all alone?

They wait thousands of years for their gas to decay.
When it's toxic enough, they bum blast it away!

Nothing about ogres is tiny or small
and they rip the biggest butt burps of them all.
These huge gassy giants can clear a whole crowd
With their powerful puffs that are stinky and loud.

Can skeletons fart if they don't have a booty?
These bone heads don't need any bums to be tooty.

They rock out so hard that their fans catch a whiff
of the gas that explodes when they're playing each riff.

Full moons bring out werewolves and they love to howl,
but their efforts to roar also make something foul.
When they take a deep breath and get ready to wail,
Start to run for your life and DO NOT INHALE!

So when you come across a monster, remember what you've seen.
It's their spooky booty tooties that should really make you scream!

Their claws and teeth are just for show, there's no need to worry.
But if you smell a monster fart, take off in a hurry!

Made in the USA
Las Vegas, NV
15 October 2024